SHATTERED SPIRITS

The Fall of Ishcairn

CAL BLACK

Tessa, Thank you so much for being a sounding board, friend, and cheerleader all rolled up into one.

CRAEBURN

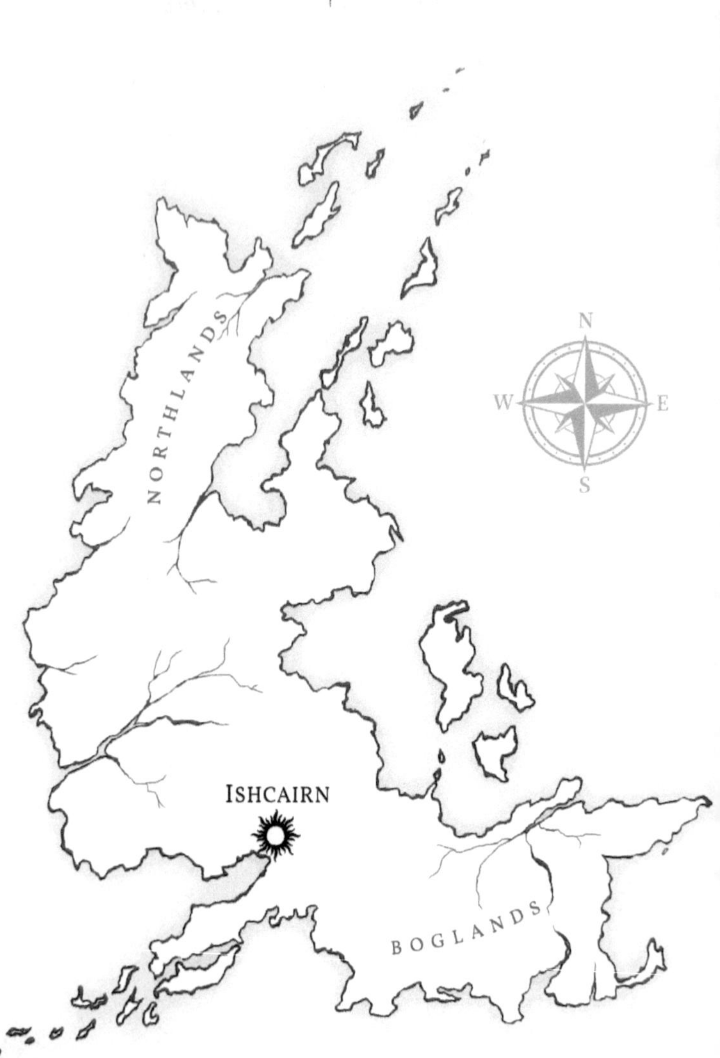

One

THE COAST

I HELD ONTO THE railing of the little ferry with white knuckles, squinting out into the heavy fog for signs of danger. Since the war began, countless ships have joined the watery graveyard that lines Craeburn's coast. Some were chewed up by the coast's jagged teeth, others hunted down by Rostaat U-boats. Rock or torpedo, the deep swallowed all ships alike. Hopefully, this one would make it to Ishcairn's port safely. We were nearly there, but the heavy fog had slowed the boat's progress to a crawl.

"Everything alright, Miss Ecksley?" Captain Murray asked. An older man, his face was nearly as weathered as Craeburn's coast. His voice was gruff, but he'd always been kind. "Been a few years since I saw you last. Don't remember you being afraid of water."

"Not afraid of the water so much as what's hiding in it," I admitted, offering the man a small smile. He used to sneak me biscuits when I was little as a treat for being such a good 'sailor' while my father pretended not to notice. I debated telling the captain that it was 'Professor Ecksley' now, but the moment had passed.

"Ah," the captain nodded, stroking his wiry moustache as he joined me in looking out at the water for a moment. "Well, reports have been clear for a while now. Seen a few periscopes, but they haven't troubled us."

"Wonderful," I said, trying to sound genuine. "Thank you, Captain Murray. I feel more at ease now." I did not, but my little lie was enough to reassure the captain. He tipped his hat and excused himself. With a sigh, I turned back to the water. The Craeburn flag barely fluttered in the breeze, the cresting wave quiet in the face of danger.

As a young girl, I found taking the ferry to be a dreadful bore. Every spring, Father would head north to organise excavations of the old barrows of the Ish'skara, the ancient people who first lived on Craeburn. As a widower, he was happy to bring his only child along as his assistant, to take notes and climb into tunnels too narrow for any full-grown man.

It hadn't been a traditional upbringing for a young woman, but we'd been happy. I had thought I'd grown out of such adventures and had a different life planned. Then the war began. Father was called to serve the Wythlands by translating cyphers. I was to take his place at Ishcairn University and oversee the desperate cataloguing and dispersal of priceless artefacts to protect them. The fighting hadn't reached our shores, but the increased U-boat presence had everyone concerned that it would only be a matter of time.

I clenched my hands around the railing to keep from reaching for the delicate chain that hung around my neck. The war had changed many things, and thinking about what could have been would only leave my ragged heart bleeding.

The cold, foggy air was a balm as I sucked it down, easing the tension in my chest. Familiar and briny, the sea was as much a comfort as it was a danger. The steady thrum of the ferry's engines underfoot had faded to a whisper as we had entered the fogbank. I knew it was dangerous to travel at speed when the captain couldn't see, but the crawling pace did nothing to assuage my fear of any U-boat lurking beneath the water.

I'd read newspaper clippings boasting about how Wythlands' ships outran the Rostaat U-boats, but there were just as many about ships that had fallen to such hubris. Surely U-boats would let a little ferry past, wouldn't they? The knot in my chest twisted again, and now the fog was too thick in my lungs.

Were we a mouse, ignored by the wolf pack? Or a lame deer trailing blood behind us?

"Tea, Miss Cornelia?"

My body reacted before I recognised the voice. I jumped, whirling on the boy who had approached, one hand on my hat to keep it from falling overboard. Poor Edwin Acton blinked, his long brown lashes matching the spatter of freckles across his nose and cheeks, both of which were scrunched up in concern. I had plenty of failings, but being so anxious was not usually among them.

He was still small, too skinny to pass for seventeen at the recruitment office, even though he'd tried several times. The latest attempt had found Edwin filling his pockets with rocks to fool the scale. It could have worked if not for the seam of one of his pockets giving way and dumping the rocks out onto the recruiting office floor. I suppose that had been the last embarrassment Edwin's grandfather would suffer. Sir William Acton, a renowned scholar and knighted for his work, gave me the 'opportunity' to bring Edwin north to Craeburn as my assistant. The way I had been my father's, and my father had been his.

It was hard enough to tell the Acton Patriarch 'no', but it had become impossible when he said the magic words.

It's what Lawrence would have wanted, Cornelia.

The thought made me sick because it was true. It was what Lawrence would have wanted: to keep his brother safe and busy until the war ended.

"Sorry Corrie, I didn't mean to make you jump," Edwin said, his large ears going red. "The captain said you would like some tea."

He'd be fifteen in a month, and he was the very picture of his older brother when we were that age. Stormy grey eyes peered out from bushy eyebrows that gave away the anxious nature of the Acton boys: always worrying. Edwin had shoved his mop of mousy curls under a pageboy hat, but a few strays snuck out near his temples. The familial resemblance that I once found so endearing now made it difficult to look at Edwin for long.

I took a deep breath, setting aside the thoughts of Lawrence and their grandfather.

"I know you didn't," I said, forcing myself to let go of my hat so I could accept one of the two tin mugs that Edwin held. Another day, a better day, and I would have pushed the brim of his cap down over his eyes like I used to. Instead, I smiled apologetically and wrapped my fingers around the warm tin. It was comforting, a ritual meant to soothe our nerves. How funny that Captain Murray had been the one to think of it, and not me.

"I was just lost in thought." I blew the steam from the tea and took a delicate sip. It was weak, but it was warm and had a drop of honey in it. A small luxury during the war. "It's been over a year since I've been back at the university, and two since I was on a dig." A quick glance at Edwin told me he wasn't convinced.

"Besides, who are you calling 'Miss Cornelia'?" I asked, lifting an eyebrow. I don't think Edwin had ever used my full name in all the years that I've known him. "You're my assistant now, not a stranger."

Edwin rolled his eyes.

"Father said that since you're not part of the family anymore, I have to use your full name," he said. His normal expression of worry pinched into a scowl that he politely directed out toward the fog. Oh Edwin, ever the little gentleman. "I don't think you aren't family anymore," he muttered. "Besides, we don't even know if–"

I cut him off with an unladylike snort. His words cut deep, but it wasn't a fresh wound. Lawrence had disappeared out on the front months ago, reported as missing in action. Sir Acton might still think I was a future granddaughter, but the news that Edwin's father no longer did was no surprise. He'd wanted Lawrence to marry a proper lady. With a dowry.

"Exactly," I said, swallowing the fresh pain. "We don't know. As far as I'm concerned, you are still my pesky younger brother." I reached out, swatting the brim of his cap so it tipped down, blocking his eyes. Edwin sputtered, the usual routine about how he was too grown for such silly behaviour.

A low clap caught my attention and for one insane moment, I turned back to glare at the cabin, certain someone had got into my luggage and dropped one of my books. I blinked, realising with a chill that the sound had come from out on the water.

Glancing back into the fog, I watched a dull violet light bloom somewhere far ahead. Even with the obfuscating grey, the strange colour made my eyes water, as though the light was brighter than my eyes could register, in colours I couldn't see. A second flash of light was brighter, and I ducked away, squeezing my eyes shut and wrapping my arm over them to shield them from any further blasts.

The clatter of my dropped tin mug was lost as a rapid series of booms ripped over the water, each louder and sharper than the last. The final crack of thunder hit me with a blast of frigid air that tore through my thick wool coat like it was nothing. My hat was ripped from my head, the pin that had held it in place scratching a line along my scalp as it went.

Gasping, I peeked out over my arm with watering eyes to see the ferry was now covered in a rime of frost. The spilled tea had frozen over, the mug now stuck in place. Wiping the water from my eyes, I straightened and looked around to see that the fog had frozen. I'd been staring at it for hours, but now the grey wall had turned into a veil of shimmering ice crystals that slowly drifted down to the water.

It was as beautiful as it was unnerving.

Ahead of us, a zeppelin fleet emerged from the falling fog, one by one. They had been impossible to see moments ago, their silver hides reflecting the grey skies above and the fog below. They hung so low in the sky that I could see the machine guns mounted along their bellies. The nearest had the black Rostaat eagle painted on its prow with its name in gothic letters. 'Sturmbrecher', the Stormbreaker.

Heart in my throat, I stepped back and grabbed Edwin's arm to drag him with me. The boy hadn't moved, and was still staring out at the horizon, his eyes bloodshot and crying pink tears. Someone inside the ferry's bridge rang the fog bell as a warning to the crew and passengers, few as we were.

"Edwin, come away from the railing," I said. He was holding onto the rail tight, and though he was still small, I wasn't strong enough to pull him free.

"Corrie?" Edwin asked, his voice shrill with panic. "Corrie I can't–"

"Yes, you can. You can let go," I said. "We need to get inside."

Edwin swung his arm out, hitting me in the chest hard. "Corrie? Where are you?" He asked, turning his head toward me. His pink tears had darkened now, and his eyes were filling with red. "Corrie, I can't see!" Edwin said, his voice breaking into a shriek.

"I can't see!"

Two

A City of Ghosts

EDWIN HAD NOT BEEN the only one blinded by the blasts. Other passengers and several of the crew had gathered in the main cabin, their eyes streaming bloody tears just as Edwin's did. Toward the back of the cabin, I saw someone tending to Captain Murray, and my heart dropped. That man loved the sea, and he'd lived his whole life on a boat. Being unable to work on a ship would destroy him.

"This way," I said to Edwin, dragging him over to where my trunk was lashed, and sat him down on the bench next to it. His wails joined those of the others, making it almost impossible to think, and he immediately tried to stand again. I pressed him back down.

"Stay still. I'm getting something to help." When I was certain he would stay, I let go and dug into my trunk for my medical kit.

I pulled out a carefully rolled bandage and noticed my hands were trembling. If I had not flinched away, would I have been blinded like Edwin? I stole a guilty look around the cabin, trying to find a common trait among those that had saved their vision. An elderly man, whose arthritic hands shook as much as mine. An engineer, still covered with coal dust and sweat from the bowels of the ferry. The first mate tending to Captain Murray. There was no common thread other than being spared by chance.

The small bottle of whisky in my medical kit clinked against my sewing tin as the ferry rolled over another wave caused by the blasts. Excavations often had mishaps. Scrapes, crushing injuries, animal bites… I'd learned to keep a small bottle on hand since laudanum was needed at the front. A hard spirit did in a pinch. Unstopping it, I took a quick swig to calm my nerves. My hands were a-flutter, and I'd be no use to anyone until I could pull myself together.

"Here, take a sip. This will calm your nerves."

I held the bottle up to Edwin's lips, and he flinched away, lashing out blindly at me. His arm struck the bottle, knocking it from my hands onto the deck. It landed with a crash that set off a chorus of screams among the blinded. The screams continued, and no amount of soothing lessened their panic.

Bewildered, I looked at the others who could still see, and in their faces, I saw hopelessness mirrored back at me. Whatever the blinded had seen, it had driven them into mindless hysteria.

"We need to dock," I shouted to the engineer. "We need help." The Celestial Father only knew what waited for us on the shore, but there were doctors in Ishcairn that would know what to do. The university's medical program was the best in the country. Surely someone on shore could help.

I don't know if he'd heard me, or simply came to the same conclusion I had. The strange blasts had cleared the fog, but how long would the clear horizon last? Within moments, the hum of the ferry's engines grew louder, and the boat accelerated toward the port.

The wails of the blinded only grew louder, more desperate. Edwin had curled in on himself, palms pressed against his bleeding eyes, as he rocked back and forth in mindless panic.

A better woman would have felt some maternal pain, seeing a boy in such distress. I felt unsettled and wrought with guilt. Something about that light had hurt to see, but I had looked away before the closer blasts. Had Edwin and the others seen something that drove them mad? Or was it such a shock to lose their sight that they were now beyond coherent thought?

I frowned. If I could find out what had happened, it might be able to help the hospital cure the blindness, insanity, or both. If I stayed, the cries of the blind would drive me insane as well.

The ferry's fog bell rang out twice, alerting the pier to its arrival. Steeling myself, I dug into my trunk for my work boots and satchel. The dainty shoes I was wearing would make walking among rubble treacherous, and I didn't want to add another injury to the catastrophe. Yanking my boots on, I laced the dusty, worn things up tight.

"Where are you going?" the elderly man asked, tottering over to grab my arm. He had to shout to be heard over the wailing, and trying to focus on what he was saying amid the screams hurt my head in an odd way. Like I was already asking too much of my mind to stay sane. "My wife needs your help."

"Not *my* help." I pulled my arm gently, but his gnarled fingers dug in to hold me fast. His bushy eyebrows did their best to hide the wild panic in his eyes. It was a struggle to be kind, but he looked as afraid as I felt. Something was terribly wrong with anyone who had seen the violet light. "She needs to get to the hospital, sir. I can get there quickly and bring back doctors and nurses."

"I'll go," the man shouted, spittle flying from his lips. His grip would have hurt were it not for the thick wool of my coat. "You stay here and tend to her like a good little lady."

"Alright." I gently patted his hand. "Best you sit with her until we dock, to keep her calm." I smiled with what I hoped was reassurance. I had no intention of staying in the cabin with the blind. I was a historian, not a nurse. I could patch up basic cuts and scrapes, but this? This was well beyond my abilities.

Once the old man's back was turned, I grabbed my satchel and hurried out onto the deck.

One wail replaced another. Sirens rose from Ishcairn, growing shriller as the ferry approached the pier. As the ferry slowed, I had to hold myself back from making a leap for the safety of the dock. I needed to get away from Edwin's wails, away from this cage of a ferry where the blind cried blood. I would get them help, yes, but I needed to stay sane in order to get that help.

Behind me, the old man shouted something. He was easy to ignore in the cacophony.

The ferry pulled alongside the pier, steel screaming and wood splintering as the hull bounced along the structure. The impact threw me forward into the railing, which bit into my hip and ribs so sharply that the air was knocked from my lungs.

A sailor came running down the pier, hat in hand, as he screamed something at us. He'd lost his woollen coat and pale dust and soot covered him from head to foot, turning him into a spectre from some nightmare as red tears ran from his left eye. Wheezing, I pulled myself over the railing and leapt onto the pier.

I crumpled the moment I landed, pain cutting deep into my side. I pressed my hand to where I was certain I'd been hit by shrapnel, but it came away clean. No fresh blood, just what remained of Edwin's, worked into the wrinkles of my palm.

The sailor leapt past me, his good eye wild with terror. He jumped for the boat's railing, tucking his feet up in an attempt to clear it. He didn't. His boot caught the very spot I had slammed into, and the cursed bit of metal swiped his feet from under him. He landed on the deck face first with an almighty crack. His legs twitched violently, but with no thought behind them. The angle of his neck left no hope for a recovery.

I stared at his body and the slow spread of red that stained the ferry's deck. More senseless death waited in the city, but something about the sailor shook my earlier confidence that the hospital could help.

What had he been running from?

Bracing a hand against my side, I swept my skirt and petticoat away from my feet and slowly pushed myself up to stand. The pier swam under me, and pinpricks of light sparkled in my eyes. I took a careful breath, blinking until my vision cleared. Lawrence would be so upset that I got hurt.

The thought bubbled up on its own, vicious in its simplicity. Lawrence had always been the cautious one, too eager to lay blame when an accident happened on an excavation. His fear of the unknown had always been infectious, worming its way into the crew until the littlest thing became a portent of disaster. He'd meant well, I know.

As I stood alone on the broken pier, watching the fog descend on a battered Ishcairn, I couldn't help but feel deep relief that he was not here. Doubtless, he would have tried to protect me and leave me to care for his screaming brother. The thought twisted into a fresh wave of guilt. Edwin had found no comfort in my presence. This was the best way to help, but logic did nothing to lessen the guilt.

I kept my hand pressed to my side and began to walk, gritting my teeth against the sharp pain. I kept a slow pace, unwilling to twist an ankle on any of the broken spars left by the ferry's impact. One step in front of the other brought me to shore, where I found the pier abandoned.

The door to the ticket booth hung open as I passed, its painted iron bars no longer safeguarding coins left abandoned on the counter. The breeze blowing the fog back ashore ruffled pages of tickets still bound in their booklet, a splotch of ink and a black fingerprint obscuring the name of whoever had been purchasing passage.

Frowning to myself, I pressed on past the booth to the board-walk that connected Ishcairn's piers to the city proper. Nestled in a stormy cove, the city was built on the slope of a dead volcano. Millenia of rain had worn away soil, leaving Craeburn's famously dark granite bare to the sky. Ishcairn was older than our oldest written records. As far as any of us scholars knew, it had been there for as long as people had lived on the island.

Now plumes of smoke rose into the sky, one for every blast I'd heard. Screams and wails rose and fell from within.

We'd taken it for granted that the stone city's position kept it defensible against attack. But the airships cared little about dangerous seas, and even less about the cliffs that had repelled so many other attempts to take the city. Why, I remember my nanny telling me stories of the old gods of Craeburn and where they were buried. She said one slept below Ishcairn, giving the city its name. Nan had said Ish sent the storms that so frequently had blown armadas off course, protecting the city from invasion.

The legend had protected the city as much as the coast had, until Rostaat had found a way over the water.

The sirens dipped in pitch before warbling away, pulling my thoughts back to the present. Blessed silence flooded my ears, and I closed my eyes and basked in it. Lawrence used to joke that I was an old man at heart. I love the hushed whispers of the university library, the muffled drip of moisture in a stone barrow. He'd say that would all change as we had children, that I would learn to love the babble of infants once they were mine. The thought still made me feel ill.

Guilt washed over me again, and I reluctantly opened my eyes. Lawrence was lost on the continent somewhere and I'd left his only brother on the ferry, blind and alone. I could get lost in thought once I'd found Edwin help.

There was a guard station just beyond the fish market. It would have a telephone to the central office. In my state, reaching the guards to ask for help would be the fastest. If it was just as empty as the pier, then I could ring for help.

I felt silly that I hadn't thought of it sooner.

The docks were abandoned, boats half unloaded with fish destined for market or the cannery. Several crates had been overturned. Gutted mackerel and packing salt spilled out across the cobblestone street and through the wrought-iron gate that divided the fish market from the docks. Old stone walls were a final line of defence against invasion, though in the last few centuries all they had done was muffle the noise of the docks from the city beyond.

Today, the walls had hidden the devastation of the fish market until I reached the spilled fish. During peacetime, the fish market would have been bustling all morning. Fishmongers would call out the quality of their catch, each trying to be heard over the others. So late in the day, the market should have been mostly empty by the time of the explosions. But as I stepped through the gate, I could see that the market had still been active before it was torn apart.

Stalls had toppled, their faded canvas awnings now shrouds for the countless bodies that lay sprawled among the wreckage. Trickles of blood ran down through the cracks between cobbles. I watched as the dark rivulets joined into larger streams, seeping their way toward me and the docks beyond. Other than the mad soldier, the bodies were the first sign of people I had found. Where were the survivors?

I might be unfamiliar with war, but I'd seen enough injuries on our excavations to know that grievously injured people were far from quiet. Yet, as I carefully made my way into the market, I heard no laboured breaths or desperate groans. Instead, I could only feel a pressure in my ears, accompanied by a sound that was as shrill as a tuning fork, but one that grew heavier the deeper into the market I went.

The fog had returned, creeping up the cobbles to break on the wall of dense tenement buildings on the far side of the square. The dark silhouette of a man moved through the fog toward me. He wasn't sprinting or screaming, a good sign.

I took a deep breath to call out, but the pain in my side bit sharply, punishing my bold attempt to shout. Instead of a hearty hello, what I managed was a pitiful wheeze as I doubled over, pressing my hands against the ribs that were certainly cracked.

The wheeze was enough. The man's head snapped toward me with an inhuman quickness. He shambled closer, his eyes pinpricks of that horrible violet light that I'd seen while on the ferry. It hurt to look at, though the utter despair on the man's face compelled me to watch as he emerged from the fog. His body was little more than a silhouette, unravelling in dark wisps of smoke with his every step. His glowing eyes were fixed on mine, pleading for help that I could not provide. They seemed to burn my vision, leaving behind smears of light, the way a flame would if one stared at it for too long. This was no man, not anymore.

His lips split, and more of that dreadful light spilled out along with a keening wail that reverberated with that steady whine I'd been hearing.

I stepped back, the hair on my arms and neck prickling with fear. I managed to blink, breaking the trance he had mesmerised me with. There were other wails joining in. Other twin sparks of violet light hovering in the fog, their bodies drifting and warping as they closed in.

Panic rose in my throat, hot and tight. I couldn't run in my condition, but something primal in my belly told me to flee. Biting my lip, I broke into a desperate trot. The guard house wasn't far, now. If I could press on through the pain, I might reach it before these wisps of people reached me. Every step jostled my ribs, stealing the breath that I needed so badly. The wails grew louder, their tone shifting from grief to something ... angry.

I wasn't going to make it. Shoving my scarf between my teeth, I bit down to stifle the whimpers of pain and started to run.

Ahead, the blue door of the guardhouse waited with its dragon head brass knocker, worn shiny from constant use. I threw myself forward, crashing into the heavy door with my good side. Built with Craeburn oak, it stood firm.

"Please," I whimpered, spitting out my scarf. I reached up and hammered on the knocker, its sharp clacks nearly drowned out by the wailing...things. I risked a glance over my shoulder. The man was closer than I'd hoped. If we both stretched out our arms, our fingers would brush against each other.

The door behind me opened, and I fell back into the guardhouse with a shriek of surprise that quickly turned to pain as I fell onto the stone floor. Something in my ribs cracked, and I tried to scream. A strong hand clamped over my mouth and nose while another grabbed onto my coat and dragged me inside. Bright spots swam at the edge of my sight, but to my deep relief, they were yellow and red, not violet.

Someone slammed the heavy door shut, and I heard the heavy iron bolt slide home. Sagging back to the floor, I let my eyes flutter closed until my vision cleared.

I was safe.

WRAITHS

"WE SHOULD HAVE LEFT her out there," a man with a softened Craeburn brogue said. It was hushed, and the howls of the smoke men outside nearly drowned it out. Lying on the cold stone, I kept my eyes closed and focused on breathing. Too deep and the broken rib stole any air I'd sucked in. Too shallow, and I would lose myself to the stars that had crowded my sight only moments ago. "She led them to us."

I tried to apologise but could only manage a whisper that went unheard.

"Are you even listening to me? You've killed us—"

"Do shut up, Henry," a woman snapped. "She's hurt." I opened my eyes to see a dishevelled woman in sensible clothes cross the guard house to where the front desk stood. Blonde curls escaped the braids pinned to the top of her head, and as she turned to glance at me, I could see the same haunted expression on her face that I was certain I wore.

"Ah, she's awake. Help her up, won't you?" the woman said. "I'll see if they have anything to help with the pain, love."

"Isn't all the morphine at the front?" The man asked. The same strong hands that grabbed me from the doorway now slipped under my shoulders. I raised my hand to stop him, but with a fluid motion, I felt myself pulled up and set on my feet.

I very nearly collapsed again from the burst of pain the movement inflicted.

"Steady lass," the man murmured, holding onto my shoulders. I blinked, turning to glare at him. Steady? He'd just been arguing to leave me out for the things outside. Years of etiquette training spoke the words of thanks that came from my mouth. I'd much rather have used some of the more colourful language I'd learned out on excavations.

"My ribs," I managed weakly, brushing my hand at his to get him to let go of my shoulders. "I'm afraid some have cracked."

Over by the desk, the blonde woman held up a dark glass vial.

"Laudanum," she announced. Striding back over to me with a swish of her skirt. It was covered with dust and blood along its hem, but it was of a better quality than any resident of the fish market could afford. "We can't stay here. If you take some, will you be able to move?"

I nodded, careful to keep my body still.

"If I can numb the pain slightly, I can lead us out of here," I whisper with a faint smile. "The fall just now jostled the injury is all."

The man behind me scoffed, his well-trimmed moustache dancing as he made a face. He was handsome in a way, though his sunken cheeks and the dark circles under his eyes suggested poor health. It would explain why he was still in the city, rather than fighting out on the front.

"I don't know if you'd noticed, lass, but there's a bunch of banshees out there," he said, flicking his eyes toward the door. "Unless you know how to get them to leave, we're stuck here."

I glanced at the door and frowned. The iron deadbolt was covered by a rime of frost that was slowly growing along the seams of the oak planks that separated us from the 'banshees'. Just like on the ferry.

"Well?" the man asked. "Can you?"

"Leave her alone, Henry." The blonde woman placed the dark vial in my hand, and I carefully unstopped it. There wasn't much left, but even a drop of the opium solution would help. I carefully let two drops fall into my mouth. It tasted sharp and bitter, burning like whiskey as I swallowed it down.

"No," I said, sealing the bottle and slipping it into the satchel that had somehow survived the journey from the ferry. "I don't know what those things are. I don't know how to stop them. But I know the Undercity." I cleared my throat, the heat of the alcohol fading into a pleasant numbness. "We can go around them."

The blonde woman leaned back against the heavy door and crossed her arms. I opened my mouth to ask about the frost, but she seemed unbothered by it. Her own wool coat was quite thick and surely kept the chill away.

"The Undercity is full of rubble and rats," Henry said, finally letting me go. I stepped to the side, bracing a hand against the heavy front desk. The edge of the pain was growing dull, and while the deep throb remained, it grew easier to breathe. Bless the guards for keeping a small stash of laudanum for themselves.

"If that's the choice to be had, I choose the rats over banshees," the woman said, tucking some of the stray curls behind her ear. She eyed me from head to toe, weary and wary all at once. "How does a southern lass like you know how to get around the Undercity?" she asked. It was a fair question. I looked like any other woman from the middle class with an odd choice in footwear.

"I'm Cornelia Ecksley, an adjunct professor at Ishcairn University," I said with as much confidence as I could muster. The words still felt odd after so long as an assistant. But the university needed to catalogue its precious archive before something like... like this happened. "I worked on local excavations with my father since I was little," I said, falling back into more familiar words. "Many of those were in the Undercity."

Ishcairn was a city of secrets, but its worst kept one was that it was a city built mostly on top of itself. The granite buildings were sturdy, and as the city grew, so did its tenements and factories. Older, smaller homes became underground vaults. Streets were bricked over to create passages used mostly for storage or unseemly business transactions. It wasn't an infrequent occurrence that brewers digging out a new vault would stumble into an old burial site or cache of the ancients. Father and I had clambered down through the old vaults to identify and remove the artefacts, leaving the owner of the land pleased to find his excavation work already done for him by the time we'd finished. We'd never found the supposed burial site of the old god Ish, however. That remained hidden.

"The Undercity is a labyrinth, but no more than the current streets," I said. I let out a shallow sigh of relief as the pain continued to seep away. "'As above, so below,' my father used to say. The guard house almost certainly has an entrance in its cellar."

The frost on the door had spread out to create a disquieting halo around the woman's head.

"Maisie—" Henry said, stepping forward. He must have noticed the frost, too.

Clawed fingers emerged from the frost, curling around the oak plank that seemed to have sprouted them. Dark, drifting black smoke, the fingers bit into the wood and the door creaked. The frost crept outward, giving way to a second hand that snagged the woman's blond braids. Maisie screamed, twisting with wild eyes to see what had grabbed her.

The hands kept pulling themselves further out of the door, a face following, a single eye socket glowing violet crowned through the oak, the rest of its horrible visage dragging itself forward toward us.

The first hand clawed at Maisie's face, those smoke-like fingers passing through her cheek as easily as they did through the heavy door.

"Grab her," I hissed at Henry. I couldn't pull poor Maisie free, but I could try to beat back the spirit, for surely this was no banshee. Banshees warned of death, they didn't cause it. The guardhouse was emptied of weapons, no doubt snatched up as the men stationed there headed out during the bombing.

An ink pot sat next to the ledger on the front desk. I grabbed it, pouring some of the black liquid onto my right hand. Henry remained rooted in place, watching as the spirit dragged a pale echo of Maisie's face from her head. It shimmered in the air but disappeared when I looked directly at it.

"Grab her!" I shouted this time, wincing as my ribs protested. But the pain was further away now, easier to ignore.

I hurried to the door and ran my inky fingers over the frosty wood. The spirit was busy with Maisie for the moment, but my hand trembled at the thought of it turning its attention to me. I poured more ink onto my hand whenever my fingers no longer had enough to paint a line.

The scientific logic I held so dear was whispering to me that this was silly, that it was wasting precious time that should be spent pulling Maisie free. Logic didn't explain the spirit that had half-emerged through the thick oak door, nor the other patches of frost that had grown along the thick granite walls around us.

I drew the last line of the sigil, an ancient symbol I knew by heart after seeing it so often on talismans on the dead ancients. A shield knot, hastily painted on the wood next to Maisie. As my fingers dragged the ink to close the circular knot, the spirit recoiled with a shriek. It yanked itself back through the door, grabbing at its face as though it had been struck.

Maisie stumbled forward, and only then did Henry hurry forward to catch her. Already pale, now her skin was ashen, blanched to pure white where the spirit's fingers had caught her. Even with the laudanum's effects, I knew I couldn't help hold her up. I would only become another invalid for Henry to manage and despite how strong he seemed, his hollowed face suggested he was far from hearty himself. Instead, I hurried to the desk to search through its drawers for a set of keys.

"'Every lock, every puzzle has a key,'" I murmured Father's favourite saying to myself to keep my composure. Whenever I'd get frustrated with deciphering inscriptions we found, he'd give me a patient smile and a wink while repeating his motto. While it had driven me mad as a girl, in the years since I had come to see the wisdom in it. Yet finding a key on its own was never enough. 'Once you find the key, you must find out how to use it.' At least the key to the Undercity would be simple enough to use... once I found it.

My ink-stained fingers would leave prints all over the desk as I rifled through its drawers, leaving behind a clue that I was here. A key to the mystery for future scholars who might ask themselves: did anyone survive the strange events in Ishcairn? I bit my lip, unsure if I wanted to break into hysterical laughter or desperate sobs. How appropriate.

Finally, one drawer I pulled open jangled and a brass ring slid across a stack of paper, several keys of different metals hooked onto it.

"There you are," I whispered, grabbing it. I flicked through the keys to the one that looked the least used. Cast iron, simply made with a small touch of rust in the crook of its teeth. There were many locks in a guardhouse, but not much reason for guards to visit the Undercity since the last riot several decades ago.

"What did you paint there?" Henry asked, glancing back at the door. Still covered in frost. The white crystals now covered the door, creeping over the ink that I'd so hastily scrawled over it.

"It's the shield knot," I mumbled. Digging into my satchel, I pulled out the little dynamo torch Father had given me before I left. I slung the leather strap around my neck and pulled the metal chain a few times. The little bulb flickered to life, lighting my way ahead. With oil and batteries so needed at the front, Father had thought it would be helpful to have a source of light that required neither. It required charging every few moments by pulling the cord, but right now, it was a blessing.

"I've seen it before. That knot," Henry said, looping Maisie's arm over his narrow shoulders. She clung to him with the woozy desperation of a dying woman. I licked my lips and prayed to Ish that she would be alright. He was dead, if he was even real at all, but he was the closest thing to help that we had now.

"It was a common amulet for the Ish'skarans," I said, gathering my skirt up in one hand. "The ancient people who founded the city. There are still some villages that bury their dead with a shield knot amulet even today. I never thought it did anything other than offer comfort to the grieving." I'd never thought spirits were real, either. "Come on then," I said, more to myself than to Henry. "History lessons can wait until we're somewhere safe."

The stairs leading to the cellar were swept and clean, but the door that led deeper into Ishcairn's belly was covered in dust and old cobwebs. To make things safer, the city had decreed that all doors to the Undercity must be painted black and always locked when not in use. That hardly stopped the ne'er-do-wells from breaking into the old vaults, but it did reduce how many children snuck in and inevitably got lost or injured.

I swept the cobwebs away from the lock with a handful of my scarf and slipped the key into the lock that was made from the same oiled iron as the key. I tried to turn it, but the mechanism must have held some rust. It rotated a quarter turn before it got stuck. I motioned for Henry to take over.

"I'll be alright," Maisie said faintly, gently freeing herself from his grasp. "If Cornelia can walk, I can too." She seemed to have regained some colour in one cheek, though the other was still as white as chalk. Whatever the spirit had done would not be easily shrugged off, it seemed.

"We'll get to safety," I promised, knowing that my words were hollow.

"Where?" Henry asked, grunting as he twisted the key in its lock. Metal ground against metal, and I heard a click from beyond the door. "That banshee climbed through the door. Where else can we possibly go that will be safe?"

"Castle?" Maisie mumbled. She frowned, reaching up to rub at the white side of her face. "It's numb." She said, glancing at me with worry. Ishcairn Castle was built at the top of the hill, and while it was certainly the safest place against a normal invasion, I wasn't sure it would be against the spirits. Granite walls built six feet thick would repel many things, but surely it had been a target of the Rostaat zeppelins for that very reason.

"The university," I suggested, reaching out to take her hand. I gave it a small squeeze of support. "It's closer than the castle, and almost as sturdy." I gave Maisie a reassuring smile. "And it's home to the best teaching doctors in the Wythlands." That much was true, but I felt a sick guilt twist in my belly. I had a selfish reason to want to get to the university. It had a trove of information that could help figure out what was happening to the city.

Every lock, every puzzle, had a key. I just had to find it.

Four

THE UNDERCITY

THE UNDERCITY WAS BLISSFULLY quiet. The air was thick with the smell of dust and mildew, but the arched passage we'd entered was free of screaming. Water dripped somewhere in the shadows, the plunk of each droplet echoing against the old granite blocks. The tuning-fork whine had finally eased, leaving behind a strange cotton-like sensation in my ears.

"Are those really banshees?" Maisie whispered, once the door to the guardhouse was shut behind us. There was no sense locking it, but without knowing how much of a mind remained after one was turned into a spirit, there was no sense in leaving the door open for them to find, either.

I shook my head, pulling the chain to keep the torch charged. Its light wasn't as bright as an oil lantern, but it was enough to see in which direction the passage angled upwards. I motioned for them to follow, using one hand to brace myself against the cool wall as I walked. The laudanum helped, but the pain was a heavy pinch in my side that kept me from moving at a normal pace.

"They are," Henry said firmly. "What else screams like that?"

"They're not banshees," I said, keeping my tone gentle. "But I don't know what they are." I tried to think of all the legends and epic poems I'd come across in my work, but my mind was thick and trying to pull up memories felt like pushing through water. "There used to be legends of barrow-wights," I said. "But they were bodies without a soul. These seem to be the opposite." Surely, if barrow-wights were real, I would have found the signs of one over the years.

"Wraiths," Maisie said. "My nan told me about them." Her words were still slurred, but her voice was steadier now. "Spirits without body, driven mad by its loss." I slowed, glancing back at her.

The torch's light reflected from one of her pale eyes, making it seem as though it was glowing of its own accord. My belly twisted, sending another shock of pain through my ribs as I struggled not to gag. Turning the torch to face down the passage and away from Maisie, I could see that her eye truly was glowing. A dim, nearly invisible sheen, but it was there.

"Are you alright?" Maisie asked, fixing that unearthly eye on me.

"Breathed too deeply, I'm afraid," I said, feigning that I was suffering from broken ribs and not the sinking realisation that one wraith might be able to create another. I turned myself back toward the path ahead, unable to hide my horror for very long.

How many wraiths had the attack created? Hundreds, surely. I had heard multiple explosions whilst on the ferry. The docks would have been nearly empty so late in the day. But higher up in the city was the cathedral and tenements where people would have been gathering to prepare supper. Ishcairn was a dense city, its streets and alleys were nearly as tight as the passages of the barrows I loved so much. If one wraith could create another by killing a living person, the magnitude of the Rostaat attack became unthinkable. Hiding until help arrived might no longer be an option.

"Where did you come from?" Henry asked. "Are there others? Men?"

Shame crept up my neck to my ears, and I was grateful that the Undercity was dark enough to hide them. Edwin was still on the ferry, along with a handful of others who had also been blinded. Now I understood why the soldier had been so desperate to get onto the ferry. He had been running away from the wraiths, not toward the boat.

"The ferry," I said, pursing my lips. "We saw the light from the blasts—" I stopped myself and shook my head. That wasn't true. I needed to be clear about what happened. "I saw only a light through the fog and hid my eyes before the later blasts, but others were not as fortunate. They were blinded, driven mad by the sight." I couldn't take a deep breath to steady my nerves, so I focused on taking slow, measured steps.

"We were lucky to have been in the guardhouse," Maisie said. Henry cleared his throat, but his female companion paid it no mind. "I'm Henry's nurse. We were out for our afternoon stroll when he became short of breath and needed a place to sit."

"I have consumption, you see," Henry said, coughing far too loudly for my liking. I stopped, turning to look at them, letting the light of my torch cut Henry's features into grotesque relief. He hadn't coughed in the cellar, nor in the dank air of the Undercity until Maisie had mentioned he was ill. His hands had been strong, and he hadn't seemed out of breath at all when he had pulled me into the guardhouse.

I suspected his malady was not of the body but was instead a weakness of character.

"Not fit for duty, you see," he said gruffly.

"I see," I echoed, glancing at Maisie. Her eye was brighter than it had been just a moment ago, I was sure of it. We would need to get to the university quickly. I couldn't run, and Henry would be too much of a coward to help should Maisie lose her mind.

"Well, don't we make a fine lot?" Maisie said with a nervous little laugh that verged on hysteria. "An invalid nurse, a consumptive, and a professor with broken ribs."

I swallowed my thudding heart and smiled at the joke. No more chatter. I would need my breath. The university wasn't terribly far, but every step of our route would be uphill.

Dim violet light caught on the edges of a cave-in ahead. Instead of reassurance, the sight filled me with dread. I motioned for

Henry and Maisie to stop, but only one of them did. A light, icy hand touched mine. Maisie had left Henry behind and had walked up to stand next to me, her eye glowing with a pale, cool light. To my relief, she had not yet fallen into madness, nor had her eye sharpened into that violet light that I found so difficult to look at.

"Do you see it?" she asked, her cold fingers clumsily curling around mine. Her voice was still slurred, but it was filled with a quiet awe. "It's glowing."

I saw the glow, but it was that strange purple that made my eyes water if I tried to focus on it. I could look at it only because most of the light was blocked by rubble, slipping out through cracks between stones. The vault that had collapsed had been a city square once, but had served as a makeshift warehouse the last time I'd been inside. The explosions must have shaken a support column loose, leading to the cave-in. Whatever and whoever had been inside was crushed, and our path to safety was blocked.

"What do you see?" I asked, rather than give in to panic. There were other routes we could take. I just had to hope they hadn't suffered the same fate as this vault.

"A star," she breathed, lifting our joined hands to point at where the rubble met what remained of the vault's ceiling. "It's beautiful."

Perhaps I had been hasty, thinking that Maisie had not yet lost her mind.

"I'm afraid I don't see any 'star', Maisie," Henry said from behind us. His coughing had continued for a while but had been conspicuously absent as we approached the cave in. "I only see a dead end."

"I see a bit of light, but no star," I said, using the hand Maisie was holding to draw the faint rays of light that cut through the dust in the air. She turned to me, her glowing eye was close enough to see the faintest of flickering where her pupil should be. I'd never been interested in the stars. I'd preferred to look in the other direction for secrets. Now, watching the pale light in Maisie's eye, I wondered if this was what stars looked like up close.

Henry disrupted my train of thought by resting a heavy hand on my shoulder. I jumped at the unwanted touch and immediately hissed as a sharp pain broke through the ebbing laudanum fog.

"Sorry, Miss Ecksley," he muttered, immediately grabbing my arm to help steady me. I wanted to shake him off and tell him it wasn't 'Miss', it was 'Professor', but I had to focus on breathing through the pain or I risked another fall. Holding onto him, wheezing in the dusty vault air, I failed to notice that Maisie had let go of my hand and was walking toward the rubble.

"Is there another way we can take?" At least Henry was asking sensible questions, even though I hadn't the breath to answer them. Instead, I pointed up. There were other passages, but the fastest route we could take was on Ishcairn's surface. The cathedral was close, and its extensive catacombs would be the easiest way back to ground level.

At least all of its inhabitants were long dead, and no longer posed a risk of turning into wraiths.

"It's right here," Maisie called out.

She had reached the rubble pile and was now climbing it toward the beams of light that radiated through the cracks.

Henry stood silently next to me, and I nudged him to say something. Very gently, he took my shoulders and pulled me away, back down the way we had come. I tried to dig in my heels, but the gentle pull made the broken rib bite deeper into my side. With a wheezing gasp, I relented and let myself be pulled away from the woman who had saved my life.

I hadn't forgotten which of the two had been ready to leave me outside to be devoured by the wraiths.

"You saw her eye," Henry whispered, his breath uncomfortably hot on my ear. "That thing made her sick."

He wasn't wrong. Maisie's eye had been mesmerising, and now that I was no longer staring at it, I could recognise how strange it was to be so drawn to the light radiating from it. Surely, I was more rational than a moth, yet a creeping dread told me that if Henry hadn't interrupted me, I would have followed Maisie's glowing eye into danger. She'd said there was a star among the stones. Did it have the same pull on her that her eye had on me? A chill ran down my back.

Cobblestones and bricks clattered as Maisie pulled them out of the pile, tossing them aside. Her eye illuminated the rubble before her, and as she turned to look back at us, it cast a beam of pale violet light through the dark dust that swept over us. Worse still, there was a spark in the second eye that was no reflection from the first, and both were rimmed with blood that rolled down her cheeks. Just like Edwin, back on the boat. His eyes hadn't held a spark at the time I'd left, but—

"Why are you leaving?" Maisie asked, her voice split into discordant notes. She tilted her head, and a ghostly version of her led the action, her corporeal body following a heartbeat later like an echo.

I stepped back, glad that Henry had pulled me away. Whatever that 'star' was that Maisie saw, it seemed to accelerate her affliction. Swallowing hard, I grabbed onto Henry's arm and tugged at it for him to follow. We had to leave before Maisie found her 'star'. I was certain I knew what she saw and had no intention of being near the remains of the bomb that had caused all this horror.

"We need to go," I whispered to Henry. "Right now." Maisie had already returned to her task of trying to clear the rubble,

"The professor finally says something intelligent," he muttered.

An ominous groan announced that Maisie's work was bearing fruit. Just not in the way she'd intended. The shriek she let out was both exultant and horrified, but at least it was short, cut off by the collapse of what remained of the vault's ceiling.

"Do not look back," I said, turning away and covering my mouth with my scarf to keep from breathing in the cloud of dust that washed over us. I could see our shadows in it, cast by a violet light that was easier to see in the darkness than it had been in the fog. Or was it that my repeated exposures had made me afflicted, like Maisie had been? The thought turned my stomach, empty as it was.

"Whatever you do," I repeated, voice muffled by my scarf. "Do. Not. Look. Back."

Five

DOOR OF THE DEAD

UNLIKE THE GUARDHOUSE, THE cathedral kept their Under-city door in good order. The black paint was carefully applied, and the brass fittings shone in the light of my little torch. Positioned at eye level, a brass knocker shaped like a skull stared me down, its dull eye sockets meant to remind me of my impending death and keep me humble. The second half of that reminder involved repentance for my sins, but after what I'd seen since arriving in the city, death and the Celestial Father no longer held the gravitas they once had.

God in his starry heavens felt impossibly remote when wraiths stalked the streets. Ish, dead as he was, felt like a more likely saviour than the deity the cathedral was dedicated to.

"What are you waiting for?" Henry asked, reaching past me to try the latch. The well-oiled mechanism clicked, and the door moved inward a fraction of an inch before it stopped. Henry's face fell, and he pushed me out of the way to kick at the solid oak. Pain exploded into starbursts, blinding me in the darkness.

I staggered aside, clutching my ribs. If it weren't for my corset, I was sure Henry's shove would have killed me. Instead, the whalebone and coutil held my broken self together as I gagged from the pain.

"It's locked," Henry said, finally giving up on kicking his way through.

I couldn't speak, but I hoped the watery-eyed glare I shot him said enough. He'd left Maisie, and he'd leave me behind in a heartbeat if he thought it would improve his chances. Right now, he still needed me to get out of the Undercity and I was going to need that leverage to survive the trip to the university.

Wordlessly, I pointed at the flap built into the bottom of the door. It was easy to miss if you didn't know what to look for. A black leather strap was nailed to the bottom as a handle, and I knew from years past that the cobblestones had been worn smooth along a very particular track.

Ishcairn was a city with little to spare, and the graveyards had long been the resting place of the wealthy. The pious and poor had few options for a respectable burial. The catacombs offered sanctuary for the dead. Bodies would be wrapped in whatever the family could afford, and the skull knocker would call an attending priest who would collect the body through the flap at the door.

Father had crouched down the day he'd shown me, holding his lantern close to the door so I could see how centuries of bodies had smoothed the stones. I remembered the way the light had glinted off his spectacles as he winked at me and told me that only the dead used this door. That any living man who tempted Fate was cursed to die before the next sunrise. The Door of the Dead, he'd called it.

Henry had paled, and he backed up, shaking his head. Sweat cut pale streaks through the dust stuck to his face, and his hands trembled as he held them up as if to keep me from throwing him to the ground.

"You go," he stammered. "I'll guard the door."

'Guard the door'. From whom? The wraiths had crawled through a door much thicker than this back in the guardhouse.

"Fine," I gasped, slowly lowering myself to the ground. The granite stones were cool under me, and I didn't dare close my eyes for fear that I might give in to exhaustion.

I lay on my back, well clear of the flap that Henry was lifting like the gentleman he was. Pushing myself along with the heels of my boots, I bit my lip and lay on my left shoulder as much as I could, trying to keep my injured side from bumping anything.

There was no mystical transition from one side of the door to the other. When I was through, I lay for a moment on the ground, looking up at the shadows my torch cast on the vaulted ceiling overhead. Someone had taken the time to etch constellations into the granite, a way to lead the spirits of the deceased up to the heavens, perhaps? I sighed, shining my torch around the vault where I now found myself. Lawrence would have known. He'd always found the stories of the Celestial Father to be fascinating. He'd been the one who liked stars. I liked dirt.

The thought of him made me sick with guilt. I should want to be trapped down here with him, my childhood confidante and husband-to-be. Yet, lying there among the dead, I knew he would be little better than Henry.

They were cut from the same cloth, men afraid of the unknown and known alike. Afraid of war, though Lawrence had gone to serve while Henry had not. The letter informing us of his disappearance had said Lawrence had disappeared in action, but I knew him. I knew that missing didn't mean he had been fighting. Missing could have meant he'd run and been shot for desertion, and his death covered up to spare his knighted grandfather's reputation. Lawrence had been terrified of thunder. The moment he heard it, he'd run to hide in the nearest cellar. It was no stretch to think he had tried to do the same during the first bombardment.

When we'd been children, I felt brave when I protected him from his fears. As we grew up, that bravery turned to suffocation. I hadn't been able to go anywhere without him until the war began. He was like a puppy ever nipping at my skirts, whining if I took a risk. Crying if I so much as suggested returning to excavations, asking 'What of our children? '

I let out my breath, and with it, the last of my guilt.

What children? I wanted to be down here, among the dead, learning their names and secrets and why so many had held amulets with the shield knot, not locked away with screaming infants.

"Miss Ecksley? Can you open the door?" Lawrence whined from the other side. No, not Lawrence. I shook my head to clear out the confusion. Henry. It was Henry, some wealthy stranger from a family wealthy enough to feign consumption to avoid the draft.

"It's 'Professor' Ecksley," I said, feeling detached from my body. Free. Still, I pushed myself up slowly to my knees, then to my feet. Each movement sent fresh starbursts alight in my vision. There was no key in the lock on this side of the door, making Henry's request impossible.

"Who cares?" Henry asked, his voice rising to a near shriek. "Open the goddamned door!"

The pleasant feeling of detachment was fading, but my misplaced duty toward Henry had evaporated. I owed Lawrence and Edwin apologies, not him.

"It's locked," I said quietly, sagging against one of the support columns. "And there's no key. Crawl under or stay there while I look for one." I couldn't bring myself to care anymore. There was a moment of silence before Henry kicked the door again, and again, building to a frenzied tempo punctuated with wordless shouts of rage.

I was so tired.

My wool coat had grown too heavy for me to manage. Unbuttoning it, I let it fall to the floor and left it behind. Henry would either save himself or he wouldn't. I was not his nurse.

I had expected the cathedral to be full of survivors and injured. What I found as I emerged from the catacombs were empty pews and red prayer candles that had burned down to the wick. I watched their flames flicker wildly as they took their last gasps of air before snuffing out.

I wanted to pretend I didn't feel like those candles, but climbing the stairs out of the catacombs had sapped what little strength I had. All I wanted to do was lie down on the cathedral's stone floor and let the granite pull the heat from me until I no longer hurt.

Vertigo struck me as I staggered out of the side transept to the cavernous nave, its lofty ceiling so far overhead it may as well have been sky. Grabbing onto the nearest pew, I dug my nails into the oak until I could steady myself. I closed my eyes to stop the room from spinning and froze.

I could see my hands.

My breath caught, hitching on my broken rib. I could see my hands even though my eyes were closed. They were faint, dying embers glowing in the darkness, but I could see them. I could see the little scar on my right knuckle from an injury I had received on my first real excavation. I'd seen a glimmer hidden through a small opening in the barrow's inner wall. I'd reached in expecting an artefact and found a rather perturbed rat, instead.

I opened my eyes, the scar remained. Faded to pure white, now, it was only visible with the way it reflected the light of the cathedral's candles. There was little doubt about it now. I was afflicted, just like Maisie was. Had been.

The vertigo passed as the cold realisation sapped the heat from my body. I had to find the key to what was causing this, or I would lose my mind just like everyone else in this damned city. The stained-glass windows were dark, telling me night had fallen outside. How much time did I have left? Not nearly enough.

Slowly, a droning chant rose out of the steady whine of noise that had returned. I hadn't noticed it at first, feeling too ill to focus on anything other than getting to a pew to steady myself. For a heartbeat, I thought the chant was part of the affliction, but glancing over to the altar reassured me it was not.

The cathedral's priests knelt around the carved marble effigy of the Celestial Father's holy flame, their arms raised in supplication. Using the pews as support, I moved closer. I knew most of the priests. I could even call some 'friend' through our shared love of Ishcairn's history. If their wits remained with them, maybe they could give me insight into what was going on.

I should have been wiser.

Drawing level with the gathered holy men, I heard their voices split into discordant tones. Some had already collapsed, lying on the steps to the altar with their arms still outstretched, lips mumbling the words of their chant. To a man, their eyes had been bleached white, made all the more disconcerting by the brilliant red that rimmed them from the affliction's bloody tears.

I watched, a hand pressed to my mouth as one of the collapsed priests shifted, his eyes locking onto mine. I recognised the violet spark in them and hesitated. Father Clement had been a dear friend in the past, but did he remember himself? Did he remember *me*?

The old man smiled, face crinkling the same way it had years ago whenever we spoke about the cathedral's history. With great effort, he pulled one hand away from the altar and beckoned me forward. If I could have run, I would have.

"Corrie," he whispered as I knelt next to him. I took his hand in mine, his skin cold to the touch despite his arthritic knuckles that had plagued him as long as I'd known him. "Darling girl, I'm afraid you've come at a poor time."

None of the other priests seemed to notice my presence, a relief. Clement was who I'd hoped to find. I gently pressed his hand to my cheek and smiled so he could feel the expression.

"Well, I couldn't let you get away with the discovery of the century, could I?" The absurdity made me want to laugh, but I was worried if I started, I might never stop. "Has the navy been—"

Clement shushed me, patting my cheek lightly.

"There is no rescue, my girl," he said, the crinkle of his eyes smoothing into deep sadness. "The telephone lines... there is nothing. No one left." His words were splitting, and he frowned, forcing them out before he lost them. "The Father is distant, his fires dim. But Ish..." he trailed off, struck by a shudder that shook a faded blue image of himself loose from his body.

"What about Ish?" The name was like a hook, catching on my mind and dragging me out of my despair. The father groaned, shaking his head to clear it. "Father Clement?"

"Not dead," he managed. "Dormant. We—" he shuddered again, his fingers curling against my cheek, nails digging into my skin. "We lied."

I carefully pulled his hand from my face, and his fingers came away bloody. I'd barely felt any pain. My affliction was progressing, and it wouldn't be long before I lost myself to madness.

"Go!" Father Clement gnashed his teeth as the affliction tore his spirit from his flesh, using the last of his strength to pull away. I scrambled to my feet, the once-sharp bite of pain in my side now dulled to a far-away ache that was deeply worrying. Did I have even less time than I'd thought?

What did Clement mean Ish was 'dormant'?

I had more questions, but around us, other priests convulsed, their faded souls no longer moving in concert with their bodies. It was only a matter of time before they were wraiths, and if I let any catch me, all hope to stop this would be gone.

Grabbing my skirts in my hands, I ran for the cloisters. Clement had an office, one I'd been to many times over the years. I couldn't risk the time it would take to search his records for a clue about what he meant about Ish. It was time to go to the source. If I was going to find out what Rostaat had dropped on us, I was going to need to examine the bomb Maisie had found. But first, I needed to shield myself from its light.

Six

KEYS

THE CLOISTERS WERE A mistake. The peaceful courtyard I remembered, dominated by a centuries-old oak, was now occupied by wraiths. A couple still held their body's shape, crouching by bodies strewn along the walkway. Others had grown distorted, their limbs too long for any human and their spines curved into a predatory hunch. Patches of frost along the outer cloister wall told me that more wraiths lurked within the thick stone, ready to drag themselves through if I caught their attention.

I could see them more clearly now. The violet light spilling out of their eyes and mouths was still uncomfortable to look at, but either it had changed to something human eyes could see, or my eyes were no longer purely human.

Whatever changes the affliction was making to me, it wasn't enough for the wraiths to think I was one of them. The sound of my laboured breathing and the clatter of my boots echoing off the granite floor caught their attention. As one, the wraiths' heads snapped toward me, their mouths gaping as they began to wail.

Plugging my ears, I ducked to my right. It was the longer route to get to the church offices on the other side, but the large and inhuman wraiths were to my left. One's arms had split into a second pair, and it was already dragging itself through the cloister's inner wall to head me off.

Summoned by the howls of the visible wraiths, shadowy hands emerged from the patches of frost as I ran past. Some dug into the stone to haul their owners through the granite, while others stretched out claws to snag me as I ran past. The affliction kept the pain of my side at bay, but my body wouldn't be able to move fast enough to avoid all of them. Especially the large wraith that had given up all pretence of humanity.

Its four arms let it move through the courtyard faster than I could, leaving frost patches on the grass as it pulled itself along. If it had once had legs, they were gone, its body trailing off in wisps of black smoke that whipped back and forth as it moved.

It caught me as I reached the corner that would have led me to safety. Just a few more feet, and I'd have been clear. Instead, it plunged one arm through the iron grate that separated the courtyard from the walkway and knocked me from my feet with a single swipe.

I tumbled into the outer wall, the broken rib's pain blazing through the affliction at the impact. For once, I didn't breathe through it, I grabbed onto it. It was an anchor to my body, and

I threw myself into the fiery agony. Pain was physical, it was human.

Eyes watering, I looked up to see the large wraith pulling itself through the iron grate, its head straining forward toward me. Between us lay my satchel, the contents spilled out onto the ground. The laudanum bottle had broken, the last of the drug seeping out into the cracks of the flagstones.

A shard of glass glinted violet, reflecting the wraith's gaping maw. I reached out, snatching the shard up. Pushing myself to my knees, I yanked the thin cotton of my blouse up past my elbow, and with a trembling hand, etched the shield knot into my forearm.

The wraith howled in fury. I bit my lip and finished the knot, blood rolling down my arm to splatter on the ground. As I connected the final line, the sigil glowed a deep blue and light burst out from me. I blinked, and the glow was gone, but the pain had returned as sharp as it had been at the pier.

The wraith shrieked, though I couldn't tell if it was in pain or in fury. Its shadowy form was scattered, blasted to shreds by the shield knot's light.

I understood why the ancients were buried with the shield talismans, now. I had thought they were to protect the dead as they travelled to the afterlife, but what if talismans were worn to keep wraiths and the affliction at bay?

My fingers, still stained black from the guardhouse's ink, trembled and prickled as life returned to them. I dropped the shard of the laudanum bottle and slowly pushed myself to my feet. Like my fingers, they protested with the pain of a hundred pins. I leaned back against the cool wall of the corner to catch my breath and steady myself. The residual laudanum on the bottle shard had turned the cuts on my arm numb already, a small blessing when the rest of my body was screaming in reawakened pain.

The wraiths prowled along an unseen perimeter. Either the magical power in the city was growing stronger since I'd painted the first knot on the guardhouse's door, or the blood I'd spilled in carving the second had made the sigil more potent. Or, as the academic in the back of my mind suggested, both were true.

Sagging against the wall, I limped toward the cloister's exit and the offices beyond. The wraiths darted out of my way, and a glance back told me that the droplets of blood I left behind were preventing them from circling around behind me. A grim satisfaction settled in my belly. This was a key, I was certain of it. But for what? That, I still had to discover.

I'd bought myself some time from the affliction, but I couldn't risk wasting any of it. I hurried down the hall to Father Clement's office, dripping blood and leaving handprints on the beautiful oak-panelled walls. If I failed, would some future academic uncover my desperate trail? What would they think I was running from?

The question triggered an avalanche more. Had this happened before? Why hadn't I found evidence of it? What did I miss? And, most importantly, *how did anyone stop it?*

Father Clement's office was kept unlocked. Keys had been too painful for his arthritic hands for as long as I'd known him. He'd also joked that no one was ever interested in stealing the birth records of the Ishcairn parish, but he'd said the church lied about Ish. I couldn't help but wonder what else they were hiding among the pages of mundane history.

I left the door open behind me as I stepped inside. The room was full of bookshelves and carefully rolled maps stacked neatly behind his desk. On it, a book lay open with his spectacles resting on top, abandoned. Next to it was Clement's journal. A splotch of ink was the only clue that his interruption had been shocking rather than routine.

My curiosity pulled me over to the desk, an ornate oaken thing that was at least two centuries old. Keeping my dripping arm well clear of the book, I scanned the pages Clement had been reading when he'd been interrupted by the bombs. The book was ancient, its pages made of parchment rather than paper. The veining of the calfskin was still visible, and the ink was in excellent condition. I wanted to sit and pore over it, studying the inks used as well as the contents of the book itself.

Biting my lip, with great self-restraint, I focused on the notes Clement had been making. His arthritis made it difficult to write, so he'd developed a cipher of his own that was easier to mark, but one that took effort to understand. Even for me, who was familiar with reading it. His hands must have ached terribly earlier. The normally smooth marks were trembling, sloppy.

HRM is worried Eagle may target cathedral in a raid. Burn all references to ???

The ink splatter covered the last word, but most of it was clear. The King was concerned that Rostaat would attack the cathedral. Anger clenched my throat, and I was overcome with a fury that made me want to scream.

They knew Ishcairn would be attacked. Why hadn't they evacuated the city? Why hadn't they warned anyone? My eyes watered, and I rubbed my clean sleeve over them to keep from ruining Clement's journal. Paper did not survive water nearly as well as parchment, and I couldn't risk losing what little information I had found to silly emotions.

I wanted to scream. They knew. And rather than save a city, they'd left it as a sacrifice to the twin gods of King and Country. I had been sent to be part of the slaughter. After all, what need would a dead city have for an adjunct history professor? None other than to keep up the illusion that the Wythlands remained unaware of the threat.

"Bastards," I hissed, scrubbing my face with the cotton of my sleeve. It came away wet and stained pink.

My tears were becoming bloody. The sight of stains made my stomach drop, sucking all the heat and anger out of me. I'd slowed the affliction, but not reversed it.

If I survived this, I would tell everyone what happened. I'd make sure that we never allowed such a sacrifi—

A sacrifice.

My heart pounding, I looked down at my bloody arm, where the cuts still oozed. Ish required sacrifice. I'd thought it was an outdated form of worship, but what if it was more than that?

Sitting in Clement's chair, I pulled open the well-oiled drawer where he kept his writing implements. In it was a small sharp knife he used to sharpen his pencil. Snatching it up, I cut off each of my sleeves, using the cotton as a bandage around my forearm to contain the bleeding. My shoulders felt bare, but propriety was long abandoned in Ishcairn. I had a feeling the wraiths wouldn't care if they were tearing apart a proper lady or not.

Wiping my hands mostly clean on my skirt, I looked closely at the old book once more. It was difficult to see at first, but a page had been expertly cut out, the remaining strip of parchment so short it was easily missed in the gutter between pages. So, where had Clement put the spare page?

A sickening thought struck me. He would have had it on him. The page he'd cut out would be tucked into the robes that his body had been wearing when he'd turned into a wraith, back at the altar. Licking my lips, I set the knife aside and reached for his spectacles.

I still had to see what the bomb was, but I was close to discovering the key now. Ish demanded sacrifice and lay dormant under the city. Rostaat had attacked the cathedral because of Ish, and they chose to launch the raid by air to avoid his legendary storms. The bombs would tell me what they had done, but not why. Did they intend to wake him through mass sacrifice?

Or kill him by severing his soul from whatever remained of his body?

Either was possible, and Maisie's discovery would be the fastest way to discover which it was. But there remained the problem of the bomb itself. It had accelerated Maisie's affliction dramatically, and I suspected it had triggered the beginning of it in myself. To be able to examine it without succumbing, I would need a way to shield myself from its effects.

In my years of excavations, I had grown familiar with other Ish'skaran symbols that were frequently paired with the shield knot. Therefore, if the shield knot had a practical use after all, maybe those did as well. It was worth a try, at the very least. I'd need something other than my skin for this, a pair of disposable eyes.

I turned Clement's spectacles over and reached under my blouse to pull the small chain free. From it hung a locket and a simple ring with a glittering diamond. Lawrence had heard the King proposed to his wife with one, and despite my protestations that the ring would catch on everything (and it did) Lawrence had followed suit.

I snapped the chain with a quick tug and tossed the locket aside. I hadn't opened it since I'd received word Lawrence was missing. I'd felt too guilty that the portrait inside only stirred relief instead of longing. The ring was what I was after. Gripping it, I used the blade of the knife to pry back one of the metal bits holding the diamond in place. With its edge exposed, I pressed the gem against the glass lens and began to etch the sorcerer's knot. It was simple, a pair of eye-shapes linked together with a square opening in the middle.

Tucked into the palms of long-dead Ish'skarans, I'd found rocks with the same symbol carved into them, the centre square worn through to create a window that let anyone who looked through it see things without being affected by magic. Centuries ago, the church had claimed the stones let them spot witches, but I was hoping they would let me look at the bomb without being ripped apart.

I sighed as I finished the one lens and moved on to the other. It was a shame the church had burnt so many witches. Maybe they would have figured out what Rostaat had done and stopped it. Instead, Ishcairn only had me. Ish help us all.

I set down the ring and slipped both the spectacles and knife into my skirt pocket.

Closing my eyes, I steeled myself for what was to come next. I prayed in earnest that Ish would accept my sacrifice, that the sigils I'd etched into my flesh and the spectacles would work. That the wraiths would let me pass. I had nothing left if this failed. No more ideas, no more keys to try.

If the King had known this attack was coming, he could have sent help. Instead, the city was abandoned. Clement had been right. No one was coming. No one to save us but ourselves. The thought was steadying. If I failed, at least I would die knowing I had done everything I could.

Lifting a hand, I could see its glow through my closed eyes. The colour had changed to a deep blue, and I wondered what I had done to myself. Opening my eyes, I pressed my hands into the desk and pushed myself to my feet.

My one consolation was that if the sorcerer's knot didn't work, I wouldn't suffer for long.

Seven

THE UNWINDING

I FOLLOWED MY OWN blood trail back through the cloister. The wraiths had gone, chasing after something or someone who was easier to catch than I was. I stopped by my satchel to pick it up and shoved what I would need back inside it. My leather gloves would help me handle the remains of the bomb. A small pick and hammer to chip a sample if the bomb had grown inert. Most important was my battered journal and pencil. If I were to fail, if Ishcairn was to fall, I wanted to leave a record of what had happened here and why.

History would hold the King accountable if I couldn't.

Slipping Clement's spectacles into the satchel to keep them from getting crushed, I shouldered my bag and made my way back into the cathedral proper.

The priests were gone, mostly. Some of their bodies lay where they'd fallen, while others had attempted to run down the aisles to reach the main doors. One was still moaning, held aloft by the giant wraith I'd encountered earlier. It had regained most of its form, growing even less human.

The thing looked at me and screamed its defiance. Then it dug its claws deep into the man's chest, and with a single great wrench, tore the priest's soul from his body. I felt the visceral rip more than I heard it. Pale and sickly, the soul writhed in the wraith's grip, dripping parts of itself as though it were blood. Instead of splattering onto the floor, each drop dissipated into smoke before it reached the granite flagstones.

Heat washed up my throat, and I retched. The mottled smoke of the priest's soul darkened to storm clouds, then to pitch as it struggled to free itself from the large wraith that was still watching me.

Casually, the beastly monster tossed the empty body to the side with such force that it crunched as it struck a support column. The corpse crumpled, leaving behind a smear of red as it slid to the floor.

My breath caught on my ribs, and I reached out to steady myself on the nearest pew. None of the wraiths had shown much forethought since the pier, but this one had wanted me to see what it could do. What it had done. Beyond madness, this was malevolence. If left unchecked, would every wraith develop into a monster like this one?

Letting the newly created wraith drop, the predatory one screamed at me one last time before it turned and pulled itself over pews with its arms, scuttling out the main doors. Doors that were now hanging open to the square beyond, revealing the gathered mass of shadows with violet embers for eyes that milled about a crater that glowed as bright as any star.

Well, I now had a shortcut to the bomb. Though getting to it would be a test of the sigil on my arm. A lighthouse could withstand plenty of storms, but sometimes the waves were too tall, too strong. They'd push over the tower like it was children's blocks and sweep away any poor soul unlucky enough to have been sheltering there.

"First, the page," I murmured to myself, already feeling the pull to head toward the crater. Maisie's eyes had been beautiful. I could only imagine what the bomb would look like.

I grabbed my arm over the etched sigil and squeezed, using the sting to remind me what was at stake. Still holding my forearm, I walked over to the altar where Clement lay, his body among the more peaceful corpses. His face was twisted in agony, but as I knelt and tried to close his eyes, I found he had already grown stiff. It seemed silly to be sad over the death of a single man when the city was tearing itself apart, but Clement had been a friend.

"I'm sorry," I whispered to his corpse as I slipped a hand inside the folds of his robe to feel for the familiar crinkle of parchment. He had placed it over his heart, his undershirt keeping the delicate material from the oils of his skin. A historian to the last.

Lips twitching in a sad smile, I pulled it free and smoothed the page out on the floor.

It was a map of the cathedral from when it was first built. Far smaller, the cathedral had been a singular building with no cloisters or offices attached. It took me a moment to realise that the rooms drawn in watered down ink were not the catacombs, but a small crypt, right below the altar of the original church.

I'd studied the records with Clement over the years, and there had been no evidence of the existence of a crypt. The catacombs were for the dead of Ishcairn, but a crypt was for the holy relics of the church. Why hide its existence? Unless...

'We lied.'

I'd finally found the entrance to Ish's burial site. It didn't matter if it was in effigy or truth, to the Ish'skarans effigies were the real thing in spirit. So too, it would be real to Ish. The original cathedral had been turned into part of the catacombs, and the gothic structure built on top of it four hundred years ago.

I slipped the page into my satchel and pulled Clement's spectacles out. Brushing off a few specks of glass from the lenses, I slipped the wire hooks over my ears and blinked. They distorted the world, making it look closer and larger than it was, but as I turned to look back out at the square, I saw only faint shadows floating there. No violet light, no screaming monsters with too many arms.

It was disorienting. They looked harmless, just shadows cast in the fog. But I had just seen one throw the body of a grown man like it was nothing. They were still dangerous, and I was keenly aware of that as I walked down the aisle out of the cathedral.

Primal instinct told me to run in the other direction. There were roads out of Ishcairn that I could take. If I was lucky, I could find a horse or something to ride until I reached the next town. That assumed the wraiths hadn't reached it before I had. I was no philosopher, but I knew the illusion of choice when I saw it. Running would only delay the inevitable. Better to steel myself now, when I was at the epicentre of this hell, than to run and need to find my way back.

Even though the etched spectacles let me see through the magic, I could feel it buzzing in the air. I could still hear the furious howls and wails of the wraiths as I descended the cathedral steps into their midst. Tucking my satchel under one arm, I held onto the spectacles with my other hand in case a wraith decided to take a swipe at me. The shield knot on my arm began to sting, and every step deeper into the mob made the pain worse.

Gritting my teeth, I quickened my step as much as I dared. Any faster and I would be unable to breathe. Any slower and I risked the wraiths overpowering what now felt like an extremely flimsy defence. But it held, pushing the dim shadows away from me as I cut through them.

My chest felt tight, like my lungs were being crushed between my fluttering heart and broken ribcage. This wasn't from the injury. I remembered this feeling from when Lawrence had knelt in front of me with his stupid ring and asked a question that he knew I couldn't say no to.

He knew I didn't want it. Marriage, children, the wifely duties of staying 'safe' in the cage of a town home far away from the barrows I loved so much. He'd known all of that since we were children, and he didn't care. He'd trapped me until Rostaat declared war. I'd hated him for it, especially for asking in front of his grandfather who owned my father's future.

I swallowed down the rising panic and kept my eyes fixed on the crater ahead. I was nearly there. I'd hated how I cried when Lawrence was announced to be missing in action, because everyone had thought they were tears of grief when they had been in relief.

The crater was before me now, a slope of rubble leading down into the vault where Maisie had lost her life. Had she felt the same relief when she'd realised the vault was collapsing? That she would never have to baby Henry again, never have to cover for his obviously feigned consumption?

I'd thought, watching her, that she had been in a delirium from the affliction, but everyone I had seen succumb to it since had done so violently, fighting it to the last. Fresh pink tears welled up in my eyes as I started picking my way back down to the Undercity. I wish we could have met in another world, one that wasn't tearing itself to shreds.

A rock shifted under my foot, and I slipped. Heart in my throat, I skidded down the slope with my feet braced far apart. I couldn't afford another fall. It was a miracle that my rib hadn't pierced a lung yet. I came to a stop at what had once been part of the arched ceiling of the vault, the larger block of stone giving me enough control back for me to finish climbing my way down. The howls above were dying away as the wraiths in the square lost interest now that I was out of their sight.

At the very bottom of the pile, a pale hand lay outstretched from under the rocks that I had just climbed down from. Scratches and blood marred the delicate skin, incurred from Maisie's mad attempt at digging out the 'star' she'd seen. I felt my belly twinge at the sight of bone, and I turned away to look down the passage to where she had been reaching in her last moment.

A shard of something gleamed ahead. It was faceted, about the size of a skull, and it flickered like fire as I approached.

I could feel the pull to pick it up and see it with my naked eyes. To see what Maisie had seen. To go mad would be a relief from the constant dread I had been living with since I'd stepped into the fish market.

Instead, I carefully pulled out my journal, my gloves, and my pencil. Placing a single page of my journal over one facet, I rubbed the lead over it to record the engravings that covered its surface. Even through my gloves, through the paper and pencil, I could feel the angry buzz of magic trying to shake my spirit loose from the flesh and bones of my fingers.

I closed my eyes, shifting to the next facet and worked by feel to create rubbings of each side I could. With the strange inner sight, I watched my blue spirit hands stain violet from the contact with the shard. A flush of relief filled me as I finished. Setting aside my journal, I picked the shard up to turn it over, only for something to bite through my glove and into the pad of my finger.

Opening a single eye, I looked down to see that the shard had the remains of a glass globe at its core that would have been about as large as my fist if it were whole. The inner surface was covered with dust, and when I wiped it, my finger came away bloody. I checked again to make sure the blood hadn't come from my finger. It hadn't, instead it was half congealed into a goopy mess. The bomb had been filled with a phylactery of sorts.

A sacrifice.

The spectacles cracked, startling me from my thoughts. Through the cracked lens, violet light seeped in. I grabbed my journal and closed my eyes, ripping the spectacles from my face before they could fully shatter and blind me. I heard the lenses crack again, and the tinkle of glass falling onto the stone floor.

With cold needling my fingers, I felt along the floor for my journal. Finding it, I tucked it under one arm and set the spectacles down against the wall. They'd given me enough time to find the shard and get my rubbings. Now they were left for the future historians as a breadcrumb in my trail.

Finding the wall, I stood and carefully stepped around where I had put the shard. I could feel it now, radiating cold from where it sat. As soon as I was past, I opened my eyes and pulled the chain on my little torch. It flickered, illuminating a grotesque figure sat against the wall not ten feet away.

Henry was slumped, one shoulder slouched forward with his arm hanging dead at his side, dripping blood from where it ended in a ragged mess just below his elbow. Even his head was tilted at an odd angle, half his face slack with its flesh torn away to reveal his teeth bare to the air. I'd hoped he was dead, but a dull violet light burned in his remaining eye.

"You left me." His words were wet and mangled. "To die."

"You should have gone through the door, Henry," I breathed. I *had* left him, but it was his own cowardice that had got him killed. "It was just a door."

"I tried to climb out…" Henry lifted his remaining arm toward the crater I had entered through, bloody drool dripping down his chin and onto his coat. The effort was too much, and he let his arm fall back into his lap. "Too many. You killed me, you …" he trailed off, struggling for breath.

Henry must have been what lured the wraiths out of the cathedral. I didn't understand why he had climbed into danger when he could have just crawled under a door. It took everything I had left in me that was kind and human not to roll my eyes. He had made up his mind, and nothing I could say would change it. I had killed him. If it brought him comfort in his last moments, so be it.

I left him again, his voice rising into the high-pitched wail of a wraith as I made my way back to the Door of the Dead. Henry was not the danger I faced right now. The affliction had returned, numbing my fingertips and stealing away the throbbing pain in my side until I felt like a ghost in my own body. I knew that touching the bomb shard would drastically shorten my life, but what other choice did I have?

The lack of pain made hauling myself through the Door of the Dead easier, though it was unnerving to feel the pressure of the granite under me but not its chill.

Safely back in the catacombs, I charged my torch a few times and opened my journal to see what Rostaat had dropped on us.

I frowned, flipping between the different pages. All were Ish'skaran symbols, ones I had spent my whole life studying. But they were wrong, mirrored. The triskelion was the most sacred symbol the ancients had. Its three spirals curled clockwise, symbolising the continuous cycle of life: birth, life, death. A sacred cycle that all beings followed, even gods. More than that, it showed the unity of what the Ish'skarans believed made up a person: body, mind, spirit. A holy trinity that sought a balance between all three aspects of existence.

The triskelion engraved onto the bomb spun the other direction, reversing the cycle. Undeath, unlife, unbirth; power flowing out from the body to unwind the trinity. Souls torn from bodies, minds torn from souls until nothing was left but mad wraiths who sought to wreak their fate onto anyone they could find.

The other symbols were to support this. Single spirals following the same direction, repeating the intention of undoing. I'd never thought to weaponise a sigil's orientation, but someone in Rostaat had.

Finally, the last rubbing was an inverted labyrinth, also mirrored. Ish's symbol reversed.

I frowned. After studying barrows for my whole life, I had only just found out that Ish was not truly dead, as Father Clement whispered his secret to me. So, who else had known, and how did Rostaat find out?

I pressed my lips together. That question would have to wait. I had an idea of how to stop the magic that was unravelling me, but first I would need to find the cathedral's crypt. I would need to find Ish himself.

Eight

THE CRYPT

THE OLD CHAPEL WAS in the lowest level of the catacombs, built from unhewn stones, expertly placed to minimise the need for grout. The newer Undercity was all blocks of granite cut into uniform bricks, with the only variation being how weathered those bricks were. Down here, every stone was unique, pulled from the dirt rather than a quarry. I let my still-numbed fingers trail over the stones as I entered the chapel's ruins.

It had been converted into a burial chamber for the original bishop of Ishcairn, credited for bringing the Celestial Father to the island. Finding Ish's tomb below the bishop's would confirm that he'd been instrumental in the disappearance of the old beliefs. How he convinced himself that a remote god in the skies was more worthy of worship than one right below his feet was something I could never understand.

The chapel was small, its walls several feet thick, and its windows bricked up by stones from the cathedral's initial construction. Cut to shape, they seemed rigid and out of place next to the original walls. There was no locked door or iron gate. So deep was the old chapel that the only people that bothered to venture down to it were the priests tasked with keeping it tidy, or historians like me.

The open doorway made me uncomfortable, and I found myself glancing back every few steps. Doors wouldn't stop a wraith, but they would slow them down. If what had once been Henry was determined to seek vengeance, the open entrance felt like a liability.

I closed my eyes and took as deep a breath as I dared. The smell of musty rot and old stone calmed my nerves. Henry's wraith would have had to navigate the catacombs to find me, first. Even if he'd retained his mind, the maze-like corridors made it easy to get disoriented.

I was alone with the dead, for now.

Pulling Clement's stolen page from my satchel, I held the torch up to it. The chapel had changed slightly since being turned into a tomb for the bishop, but his sarcophagus was placed where the altar had once stood. The original crypt was drawn below, but not where the stairwell had been hidden.

Of course.

I shone the light around the chapel, but other than the bricked in windows, there were no obvious doorways. The windows were easy to discount. I'd been on the other side of the old chapel's walls, where more priests were laid to rest. There were no secret passages there. What I was looking for had to be within the chapel itself.

I approached the sarcophagus and eyed the thick marble slab that sat on top. It had been carved into the bishop's likeness, though time had worn down his features to an anonymous death-mask. The metal sceptre he clutched was regularly oiled by the priests to prevent the relic from rusting away.

This was the most likely solution. Hiding the stairwell under the body of the holiest man in Craeburn would ensure that no one ever found Ish's tomb.

My small pick and hammer wouldn't be enough to break into the sarcophagus to see if I was right. If I had had a dig team with me, we could have levered the marble from the base with no damage. But not only was everyone else in the city mad or dead, I couldn't waste time being delicate with obstacles in my path.

I looked at the sceptre. It was solid metal, more like a mace than a relic, really. It would have to do.

It felt wrong, wrapping my hands around the upper shaft of the sceptre, but the pain in my ribs had faded away to almost nothing. I had precious little time left. Maybe even minutes instead of hours.

Taking another deep breath, I planted a foot against the marble shoulder of the bishop and heaved. I felt something give in my side, and immediately the pain was back, hot and thick in my lungs. Letting go of the metal, I bent over as my body coughed up a splatter of blood.

Looking at the dark spots on my glove, I knew I wouldn't be able to wrench the sceptre free. Even if I was uninjured, I just wasn't strong enough.

Scowling at the stupidity of my original plan, I cast about for a loose stone. Granite was far harder than marble. I should have just smashed the carved hands first, but it was getting difficult to think. Spotting one sitting in the front corner of the chapel, I stalked over to snatch it from the ground.

As I crouched to pick it up, I felt the faintest breeze ruffle the hair by my ear. My annoyance evaporated, and I ripped my glove off, holding my hand up to the wall to feel where the breeze was coming from. The rock I had spotted had fallen out from a narrow patch where the grout was crumbling. While there were more rocks behind the empty space where the fallen one once sat, I felt the slight movement of air once again. As if it were breathing.

I pulled out a small metal pick and hammer from my satchel. Placing the pick as deep into the grout as I could, I worked to clear it from around the stones near the ground. One fell free, then another that nearly crushed my foot, landing a hair's breadth from my toes. I had to cough out blood between stones. Each time, there was a little more red and a little less pain.

"Ish," I said, feeling the need to speak with someone about what was happening. Anyone. "If I die before I actually find you, I will be greatly displeased." It was such a mild statement for the way I felt that it left a bad taste in my mouth.

Ish didn't care about propriety. He'd been dead or near dead long before ladylike manners had been invented.

"Furious," I corrected myself, abandoning the pick and hammer as more stones came away. They were easier to pull out with my hands, creating a little tunnel that reminded me of the Door of the Dead. With every rock I removed, the breeze grew stronger. I could smell the salt of the sea now, though it was stagnant, just like the rest of the chapel.

I pressed an ear to the stones, listening for any creaks or groans that would signal instability above the small tunnel I had made.

It wouldn't matter if the stones were unstable, though. I had to go in. If I was going to die tonight, I was going to do it by finding the lost barrow of Ish. Me, Cornelia Ecksley. Not my father, Lawrence, or his grandfather. Just me, alone.

Fuelled by a flush of energy, I crawled through the tunnel on my belly to emerge at the top of a narrow, winding stairwell. The steps were remarkably unworn. In the cathedral, centuries of footfalls had worn paths into the granite down the aisle and on the steps leading up into the ruins of the old building. But here, the steps were flat, the grit of the stone matching those that made up the walls around me.

I started to descend, but stopped on the third step. My torch had gone out while I'd crawled through, and I hadn't noticed. Bracing myself against the outer wall, I blinked.

I could see. A dim blue glow lit the stairs from below, but I knew in my heart that it shouldn't be enough to see by. Pulling my bandage off my arm, I looked at the shield knot I had etched there. It, too, seemed to glow that same dim blue.

"Ish, I hope this is your doing and not the bomb's," I muttered. When I coughed again, this time I felt the sharp jab of broken bone press into my side.

Spitting the blood from my mouth, I descended further to find the remains of a wooden door, the weight of its iron lock pulling the rotting wood from its frame to rest at the base of the steps. I charged my torch to see if there were any remaining engravings on the wood, but the light was too bright and stung my eyes as the little bulb illuminated.

I covered it with a hand, eyes watering from the momentary glare. Wiping away the pink tears, I crouched and gently touched the wood. It crumbled to dirt at the lightest touch. I left it, stepping over the remains and down a narrow passageway whose floor continued to slope down deeper.

The blue glow grew brighter, the deeper I went. I spotted luminous lichen growing along the walls which were no longer brick but hewn from solid stone dripping moisture.

The passage began to twist and turn, and I realised it was cut in the path of an inverted labyrinth, every turn taking me deeper under the city. I'd found them in barrows in the Northlands, but those were small, cut from the earth in meadows and paved with river stones. Not a maze, with deceptive paths that would lead the unfamiliar wanderer astray. These were true labyrinths. They were a meditation, the physical steps of a spiritual journey toward inner harmony.

Like the triskelion, the labyrinth was designed to bring the wanderer inward to a peace found by balancing one's body with their mind and soul.

Every step I took jarred the pain back into me. Tears streamed down my face as pain filled me with fire, but I kept walking. First one hand braced against one side of the passage, then I needed one against each wall. My breaths turned to choking gasps as blood filled my lung.

After the affliction's numbness, this was torture. Every nerve was waking up to needle at me, from the tips of my nose to the ends of my toes. I couldn't stop. I knew if I did, I would never get back up. I would die there, in the labyrinth, with nothing to show for everything I had been through since the ferry. I would mean nothing, my death would mean nothing, and no one would ever find out that the King was complicit in the death of Ishcairn.

One foot, then the other. My breaths grew quick and shallow, lips tasting salt and copper as tears ran down my cheeks and blood bubbled up my throat.

One last step, and I staggered out into a circular room with a well at the centre. Its walls were low, barely knee height and made with jagged shards of granite that looked to be cut from the walls around me. Falling to the ground, I spat out blood and panted. My tears splattered the floor, falling on sigils carved into the granite under me.

The ground trembled, and I looked up to see the surface of the well rippling. Illuminated from deep within, I dragged myself over on hands and knees to see what was below.

Stars burst behind my eyes. The pain was somehow worse than it had been when I'd collapsed at the end of the tunnel. Blinking and rubbing them away with my sleeve, I held my breath to keep the agony at bay. Blood and tears still dripped into the water, despite my effort to keep from fouling it.

An eye opened below, luminous and blue. It was entrancing, its iris flecked with green and yellow, that shifted as the horizontal pupil dilated and narrowed as it looked back up at me. The makeshift well's wall slipped under me, slicing my palms and tipping me forward.

I hit the water and understood. It was cold, stinging every cut and scrape on my battered body. Cleansing it the way the labyrinth had cleansed my soul of the affliction.

Ish demanded balance, but in the millennia that he had been dormant, the world had lost its way. Looking to the nothingness of stars for guidance while ignoring the effects our lives had on the ground we lived on.

Ish demanded humility, but even I had thought to use his existence for something so petty as social acknowledgement. I wanted to be seen as more than just a wife or mother, more than property. I couldn't save myself, but I could save the rest of the Wythlands from suffering the same horrors that Ishcairn had.

Ish demanded sacrifice. I closed my eyes as saltwater flooded my lungs and I gave it to him.

Nine

FOR GOD AND CITY

I HADN'T EXPECTED TO dream after death. But I soared over the lost city alongside other gulls, wind ruffling my white feathered wings. I banked to get a better look at the city below. The sun was rising, turning the fog pink and gold, as though it were the start of any other day.

The ground heaved up, and with a squawk I flapped harder to gain more distance from what was happening. It was a scary thing, making my little bird heart thud rapidly in my chest.

The city below trembled, buildings toppling as the god that lived below awoke. Deep rumbles and explosive cracks tore through the air. Higher now, I could barely see the city through its fog. I wheeled, watching buildings sink out of sight, replaced by a heavily muscled tentacle that curled up into the air before disappearing back into the fog. A second tentacle wrapped itself around the remains of the cathedral's spire, crushing it as though the stone were nothing.

The smell of salt and sea filled the air, the way a coast should smell. The god pulled himself from his tomb, his muscled back and shoulders gleaming in the early sun. Pale skin bloomed as coloured dots on his body expanded, turning him deep blue with glowing rosettes of yellow that lured in unwary predators.

I followed his path as he crashed down through the city, knocking down the tenements that had withstood centuries of storms.

How foolish humans had been to assume Ish was like them, I thought. He was magnificent, the very mountain that Ish-cairn had been built upon, while humans forgot about him and poured shit and oil into the waters he breathed.

The sea did not forget, and it welcomed his return with eager waves that swept over his tired skin. I swooped lower, watching as Ish swept into the cove, taking the water with him as he swam out to deeper waters.

The sun was burning off the fog, slowly revealing the devastation left by the awoken god.

What hadn't fallen into the deep cave that once held Ish had been flattened by his emergence. The wails that had filled the air all night were silenced, leaving only the rush of water as Ish's bulk pulled the sea out in his wake, exposing ancient shipwrecks that littered the ocean floor.

When it flooded back, it would wash what remained of the city clean.

I didn't need to watch.

Something heavy struck my back, and I coughed, gagging on the seawater I vomited up. Blearily, I looked down and saw the wooden floor of a lifeboat. It smelled like fish and salt and unwashed men.

"My god, she's alive!" A man, his voice thick with the north-lands brogue but speaking without the discordant echoes of the later stages of the affliction. "Not every day you pull a mermaid from the water, eh?"

I coughed again, my hand reflexively reaching for my side only for me to realise there was only a dull ache of an injury long healed.

"Easy now, easy," powerful hands gently helped me up to my knees, holding me until I waved a waterlogged glove to show that I wouldn't fall over. Sitting, the men, for there were two, helped me steady myself.

"I died," I mumbled, squinting against the bright sunlight of midday. The light seared my eyes, making them water.

"Almost," the older man agreed. His skin was dark from days on the water, his beard and eyebrows bleached white from sun or age. I couldn't tell. "We've been searching the flotsam for survivors all day, but you're the only one we've found."

I looked past him to the water. It was filled with debris. Wooden doors, broken furniture, dead animals and shattered spars of boats that had been torn apart.

My head was thick, and none of this made sense. I had died, drowning in the well that led to Ish. Hadn't I?

"Go on, start rowing," the old man said. The younger one, skin an angry red darker than his hair, nodded and stepped out of view. Soon, the boat lurched forward as the sound of oars dipped into the water.

"Where am I?" I asked, holding a hand up to shield my eyes from the sun. It was still too bright.

The old sailor thumped his foot on the wooden bottom of the lifeboat twice.

"You're floating in what's left of Ishcairn," he said, his face growing sombre. "The Queen Florence couldn't reach command, so it came to the cove to find out what happened. It looks like the entire city exploded." His pale brows knit together. "Don't you remember what happened?"

I did, but the sunlight was so bright that I couldn't think of how to explain. I was desperately thirsty and eyed the water that slid past us. It was salt. It would drive a person mad if they drank it. I knew that, but I felt half-mad already.

"Stop!" the old man shouted. I was still watching the water as a trail of bubbles streaked past.

Following it, I watched the torpedo strike a large steamship anchored in the deepest part of the cove. The ship bucked in the water and I felt the blast in my skull, a crushing pressure followed by an aching void.

I groaned, grabbing onto my head with both hands. The sun was too bright, and I could feel something moving at the mouth of the cove.

On the lifeboat, the men were shouting at each other about whether they should row to their vessel or wait. Already the steamer was listing, black smoke boiling out of the hull.

The sky grew dark as the wind changed. Cool air blew in from the ocean, driving clouds to block out the sun. As the glare faded, I watched the water boil near us as a Rostaat U-boat surfaced. Even though it was smaller than I'd thought, the tower still dwarfed the little lifeboat I sat in.

The sailors seemed oblivious to the darkening sky, instead shouting obscenities as the U-boat's hatch opened. A trio of soldiers climbed out. Two held rifles, but they were pointing in the wrong direction.

The third Rostaat sailor barked orders to surrender, saying that they would leave the men alone if they handed me over to them. 'The survivor', the officer called me. His eyes were scared, glinting with false bravado as he ordered me to come aboard.

I did, once the lifeboat had rowed over to the U-boat's deck.

"You were in the city?" The officer asked, looking too closely at my eyes.

I nodded, glancing out toward the open ocean. The steamer was abandoning ship, sending men out in lifeboats. But beyond, a wave was rolling in.

"You will be treated well, but we will need to ask you questions."

The officer was still talking, but I barely heard him over the rush of water. I pulled my gloves off and looked down at my hand. The cuts from earlier were simply white scars now, but what was concerning was the thin skin that had grown between my fingers. The ink that had stained my skin seemed to be part of me now, staining even the thin webbing. The affliction from the bombs was gone, but something else had taken its place.

The officer shouted something and grabbed my wrist, holding my hand up so the others could see.

It was too late.

The wave reached the steamer, swamping the lifeboats and capsizing the ship itself. It kept rolling forward. I was now certain the unwinding bombs were meant to kill Ish. Instead, they had led me to do the opposite. I had thought he would save Craeburn, but as I watched his wake approach, I wondered if I had misunderstood the purpose of the labyrinth being inverted. An upright labyrinth was a pilgrimage. What if an inverted one had been a trap designed to hold a god at a safe distance?

What better way for the ancient Ish'skara to protect themselves than to enslave a god?

"Wrong key," I whispered.

Acknowledgements

Thank you to Tessa and Flo for reading the early draft and helping me pick apart what wasn't working. Thank you Bird the Cat for supervising this novella from start to finish and especially thank you for not deleting any of this one. Thank you to the reading and writing community, but especially to Jamedi, Trin, Shaggy, Andrew's Wizardly Reads for being excited for this book even when I was hit with the self-doubt blues.

Thank you, Sue Bavey for proofreading and being so patient.

Lastly, thank you to my family for being the grounding and loving people you are.

www.ingramcontent.com/pod-product-compliance
Lightning Source LLC
Chambersburg PA
CBHW051234210726
48290CB00003B/956